Isabella's Treasure

Empowering Children with Body Safety

SCHOOL EDITION

Cindy L. Smith

Author of *Whispered Truth*

Illustrated by Olivia Soloria

Living Hope for Today

PUBLISHER

Isabella's Treasure
Empowering Children with Body Safety
School Edition

Text © 2020 by Cindy L. Smith

Illustration © 2020 by Olivia Soloria

Publisher: Living Hope for Today

www.livinghopefortoday.org

Editor: Nancy Shockey

Page Design: Cynthia D. Lanning

ISBN: 978-1-7324634-5-5 (hardback)

Library of Congress Control Number:2019913590

1) Child Sexual Abuse Prevention 2) Human Body 3) Health 4) Children's Empowerment

Book may also be purchased in bulk from Living Hope for Today, go to the website, *www.livinghopefortoday.org*

Printed in the United States of America

Dedicated to my wonderful grandchildren:

Justin, Kyle, Adilynn, Everett, and Hannah.

Love you - Memaw

Dear Reader,

In my 20 plus years as a school counselor in a public-school system, I thought I had heard it all. From divorce, to the child living with an alcoholic parent, to a child telling me about a judge giving her mommy "a special outfit to wear," to the student whose mom was murdered in a stairwell, to the abused child—mentally, physically and/or sexually. I never knew what a day might bring. Those kinds of days did not happen often, but when they did, they were intense.

But now, every time you turn on the television, you hear about a child currently being abused or an adult dealing with a past incident of abuse. The sad fact is that in many of these cases the perpetrator was a trusted person; a relative, a friend, a clergyman, an educator or someone with power over the child.

Honestly, it makes me so sad and angry to hear what is happening to some of our younger generation. I'm so grateful that Cindy Smith wrote this book for children on sexual abuse, so we can empower our younger generation to stand up and say "NO" to someone who is trying to hurt them.

This book is a hands-on type of book that gives excellent factual information on what a child should do or say. It's a hard book to read, but it is one every child should have read to them and discussed with a caring adult. We need to let our children know that it is okay to say no to an adult even if the adult says something different.

I recently heard a psychologist on television say when a child is sexually abused, the child does not have the words to express what happened or what might be happening. It is my hope and prayer that this book will be the first steps in giving those children the words they need.

If this book saves just one child from being sexually abused, then it has been so worth it, so the child does not have to go through the agony and turmoil of what an abused child suffers for the rest of their lives. And for those of you that are reading this book to your child, and you have been abused yourself, it's never too late to get the help that you deserve.

Thanks Cindy, for a job well done.

Joan Halloran Lippert
Retired School Counselor/Educator

Nellie walked down the path from her cottage beside the Babbling
Brook that led into a delightful place of treasures.
She heard the Brook sing,

"You are so special and greatly loved!"

Nellie sat on a rock and listened to the beautiful tune.

Nellie heard a sneeze and a familiar buzzing sound.

She looked up to see Isabella, the wisest fairy in the forest, flitting around her tiny home in the tree.

Isabella sneezed again and tumbled down, bouncing from leaf

to leaf and landed on the rock right next to Nellie.

Isabella giggled, "Sneezing made me lose my balance. My, that was a bumpy landing!"

"Oh, Isabella! Did you hear what the Babbling Brook sang to me?" Nellie exclaimed.

"I sure did! You are one of a kind, so special and loved.

I have some jewels during our journey that will give you wisdom and help keep you safe," said Isabella.

She flitted off the rock and flew in front of Nellie.

Pixie dust sprinkled out of Isabella's hair as she pulled a jewel out.

"This jewel is marked with an X and it will remind you that your body is special."

"Anywhere you can make an X with your arms is the X Zone.

Isabella handed the jewel to Nellie, took her arms and made an X on different parts of her body.

This is the private part of your body that no one should touch."

Isabella wants you trace the X Zones that she showed Nellie, with your finger on the page.

Then she added, "And no one should ever ask you to touch their body in the X Zone."

Now Isabella wants you to show her how you can make an X with your arms against your body.

"Why would that happen?"
Nellie asked.

"Not everyone is kind to children.
Sometimes people hurt children, even
someone they know and love,"
Isabella explained.

"And if anyone asks you to keep a secret about your body, it is a sad secret. Good secrets have a happy ending, like a secret about a birthday party. Sad secrets should never be kept quiet," said Babbling Brook.

Isabella pulled out another jewel from her hair, "This jewel has an Ⓢ̷ on it to remind you not to keep secrets that make you sad."

"If someone ever tries to hurt you, say 'NO!' and tell someone what happened, like your teacher or a parent."

"Nellie, who could you tell if someone hurt you?" asked Isabella.

Nellie smiled, "I could tell my mommy and papaw—they love me."

Isabella wants to know who would you tell if someone tried to hurt you?

Isabella gave Nellie a jewel with an N on it so she would remember to say "NO!" and to keep telling until someone listens.

"Telling the truth always keeps us safe. Keeping a body secret harms us," said the Babbling Brook.

Nellie said with delight, "Oh my! Look Isabella, we have arrived at Butterfly Meadow!"

But Isabella was flying away.

"Bye for now Nellie! It's time for me to shine the moon. Remember all I have taught you, for you will need it to teach others. Many Colors will guide you on the rest of your journey."

A big colorful butterfly landed on
Nellie's shoulder.

His large, kind eyes were filled with
love for her.

As he wrapped his wings around Nellie,
Many Colors said,

"Hi, Nellie. The Babbling Brook sent me to help you
for the rest of your journey!"

Nellie looked down the path and saw Ollie.
He was sitting in the middle of the meadow
surrounded by flowers and butterflies.

Nellie and Many Colors heard him crying.
The butterflies were cooing gently, trying to make Ollie feel better.

"Oh Ollie, why are you so sad?" Nellie asked, with Many Colors hovering above.

Ollie whispered, "My uncle tickles me.
He touches me in places I don't like.
And he takes pictures of me. It makes my
tummy hurt."
What Ollie said made Nellie sad.

"I don't want to.
I'll just stay here
forever,"
Ollie said.

She sat down next to him. "Maybe if you went
home you would feel better."

Many Colors flew down to Ollie and asked, "May
I give you a hug?"
Ollie nodded yes.
He wrapped Ollie in a cocoon of color.
Ollie smiled and let out a big, loud, buurrp!
Nellie giggled at the sound.

"I'm sorry this happened, I know you feel sad, but it will be dark
soon and you can't stay in Butterfly Meadow all night."

"I'm scared to go home; my uncle might be there.
When he hurts me, he says, 'it's our secret' and
not to tell anyone."
Ollie started to cry again.

"Any secrets that make us sad are secrets we should not keep.
This jewel will remind us."

Many Colors handed Ollie the X Jewel
and told him, "When someone hurts you
and asks you to keep a body secret, it is
not your fault.
You did nothing wrong."

"Ollie, let me show you what Isabella taught me.

Anywhere you can make an X on your body with your arms is the private part of your body.

It's called the X Zone, and no one is allowed to touch you there," said Nellie.

Nellie wants you to show Ollie where the X Zone is on your body.

Ollie felt good that he could tell Nellie his sad secret and she believed him and didn't think it was his fault.

Many Colors said, "Ollie, it is very important to tell an adult about this sad body secret.

And if they don't hear you, keep telling until someone listens.

Who do you love and trust, that you could tell that you have been hurt by your uncle?"

"I love my dad he takes good care of me! I can tell him," Ollie said.

"I'm glad you can tell your dad! Is there anyone else could you tell?" Many Colors asked.

Ollie thought for a moment. "I could tell my friend's mom or my teacher."

Ollie tooted.

Nellie snickered, "My, you make a lot of loud noises!"

Ollie looked embarrassed, then laughed.

Isabella flew across the meadow towards Many Colors.

"Nellie you have taught Ollie well!

Ollie you are so BRAVE to tell Nellie what happened—you are my Hero!"

"I have one more jewel for you.
It is marked with a T to remind you
to Tell Someone what happened and
Keep Telling
until they listen."

"We will all go home with you, Ollie, and make sure you are believed and protected!"

Ollie and Nellie walked down the path to his cabin at the edge of the meadow while Many Colors and Isabella hovered above.

The Babbling Brook smiled at all of them, knowing Ollie was with good friends who would comfort him and help keep him safe.

X Zone Anywhere you can make an **X** with your arms is the private part of your body that no one should touch.

And no one should ever ask you to touch their **X Zone.**

 **ad Secrets about our body should not be kept**

Say **No** if someone tries to hurt you

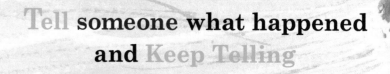

Tell **someone what happened and** Keep Telling

Letter from the Author

Thank you for taking the time to read *Isabella's Treasure: Empowering Children with Body Safety* to your child. My goal was to create engaging characters and to make the story interactive so that understanding what abuse is, and the things children can do to stay safe, is remembered.

Nellie's name means "shining light." Adults need to shine a light on this dark subject so our children can be protected.

Isabella's name means "devoted"; she teaches Nellie body safety with 4 Jewels that will empower her to stay safe. In the story Isabella is devoted to empowering children with knowledge.

The Babbling Brook is always in the background bringing truth into our lives.

Many Colors is the gentle, encouraging, spirit showing love to Ollie, a hurting child.

Nellie finds Ollie in the meadow crying because he has been hurt by his uncle. She teaches him what she has learned so the abuse will stop. Ollie's name means "kind and honest." Children are honest when reporting abuse and need to be believed and supported.

When children don't know the words they need to even express what is happening to them, they can act out in anger. Instead of asking what is wrong with a child we need to start asking what has happened to this child.

I cried constantly in first and second grade. I desperately wanted to talk to the school counselor when I walked by her office in 1966, but I didn't have the words to tell her what I was experiencing.

We can empower children with knowledge so they can find the words to tell what is happening when they are being abused. But more importantly we can give them the tools to stand up for themselves before potential abuse happens, or in the midst of abuse, so it does not continue.

It takes being brave to talk about the taboo subject of child abuse, one that is generational in a lot of families, but it will never change, and children will not be protected, if we don't speak up and start this conversation with children and adults alike. Not talking about it won't make it go away and only gives power to the darkness.

Cindy L. Smith, Author
Thriving after childhood abuse

#StopAbuseKeepTalking

More than Statistics—Child Abuse

The United States has one of the worst records among industrialized nations, losing on average between four and seven children every day to child abuse and neglect!

• 85% of sexually abuse is perpetrated by someone within the child's social sphere—for example, a relative, a family friend, a teacher, youth worker, religious leader, or neighbor.

• 1 in 4 girls and 1 in 6 boys are sexually abused by the time they are 18.

• More than 90% of child sexual abuse victims know their attacker.

• In one study, 80% of 21-year-olds who were abused as children had at least one psychological disorder.

• Around 80% of child abuse fatalities involve at least one parent as perpetrator.

• As many as two-thirds of the people in treatment for drug abuse reported being abused or neglected as children.

• 14% of men and 36% of women in prison in the USA were abused as children.

The statistics above were reported from: Bureau of Justice Statistics, Department of Justice, U.S. Department of Health and Human Services, Child Help, *Sexual Assault of Young Children As Reported to Law Enforcement* by Howard Snyder, U.S. Department of Health and Human Services

Watch for Adults Who

• Make you feel uneasy...even if you can't put your finger on why

• Refuse children privacy or invade their privacy

• Insist on physical affection even when the child looks uncomfortable

• Insist on "special time" alone from other adults and children

• Spend a lot of time with children instead of adults

• Buy children expensive gifts for no apparent reason

• Appear to put a lot of effort into getting close to children

• Have had previous allegations against them before

• Your child or other children seem afraid of

• Your child or other children do not want to be alone with

Questions to Ask

- Ask organizations about criminal background checks, references.

- Ask about training of staff / policies if suspected abuse.

- If a child seems uncomfortable, or resistant to being with a particular adult, ask them why. Be persistent.

- If an adult is taking a child on an outing, make sure to get specifics of it. Ensure they know that you are the type of parent who asks questions!

- Always make a point of asking your child about their day. Use open-ended questions, and be persistent if they seem reluctant to give answers.

- Think about whether activities would be preferable in a group. Ask why an activity is one-to-one.

Signs to Look for:

Behavior Changes

- Being excessively clinging or uncharacteristically crying when you leave

- Having difficulty sleeping: having nightmares or fear of the dark

- Returning to immature behaviors: sucking thumb, bed-wetting

- Problems at school: discipline issues, poor attention, bad grades

- Fear of a specific person or place. Isolating themselves.

- Being "too perfect" and too well behaved; quiet, desperate to please

- Radical mood swings

- Being evasive when asked questions, or having memory loss

Health Issues

- A change in eating habits; eating too much / too little

- Incontinence

- Self-destructive behavior: head-banging, alcohol use, drugs, genital mutilation

- Genital discomfort, bleeding, irritation, redness, itching, discharge, odor

- Persistent urinary tract infections

- General complaints; chronic headache, stomach cramps, sore throat

- Depression / anxiety / suicidal ideation

Inappropriate sexual development / behavior

- Excessive genital touching or masturbating in public

- Non-age appropriate language, sexually graphic

- Being sexually precocious and sexually suggestive

- Secondary sexual characteristics; covers up, wears baggy clothes

- Stops wearing make-up, stops washing, puts on weight

- Fear of undressing or refusal to undress in gym class

- Initiates inappropriate sexual contact with other children

"Molesters Do Not Wear an Ugly Mask. They Wear A Shield of Trust."

—Patty Rase Hopson

What to Say to Children/Adults Who Have Been Abused:

I HEAR YOU   I BELIEVE YOU

YOU ARE BRAVE   YOU'RE NOT ALONE

A CHILD IS NEVER RESPONSIBLE

FOR THE ACTIONS OF AN ADULT

YOU HAVE A SPECIAL STRENGTH

INSIDE OF YOU

I'M SORRY THAT

HAPPENED TO YOU

I'M HERE TO
LISTEN

CPSIA information can be obtained
at www.ICGtesting.com
Printed in the USA
BVHW092212211019
561709BV00001B/2/P